OUTPOST ON IO

by Leigh Brackett

OUTPOST ON IO

Start Publishing PD LLC
Copyright © 2024 by Start Publishing PD LLC

All rights reserved, including the right to reproduce this book or portions thereof in any form whatsoever.

Start Publishing PD is a registered trademark of Start Publishing PD LLC
Manufactured in the United States of America

Cover art: Shutterstock/Taisiya Kozorez

Cover design: Jennifer Do

10 9 8 7 6 5 4 3 2 1

ISBN 979-8-8809-0954-4

In a crystalline death lay the only release for those prisoners of that Ionian hell-outpost. Yet MacVickers and the men had to escape—for to remain meant the conquering of the Solar System by the inhuman Europans.

MacVickers stopped at the brink of the dark round shaft.

It was cold, and he was stark naked except for the silver collar welded around his neck. But it was more than cold that made him shiver and clamp his long bony jaw.

He didn't know what the shaft was for, or where it led. But he had a sudden feeling that once he went down he was down for good.

The small, round metal platform rocked uneasily under his feet. Beyond the railing, as far as MacVickers could see to the short curve of Io's horizon, there was mud. Thin, slimy blue-green mud.

The shaft went down under the mud. MacVickers looked at it. He licked dry lips, and his grey-green eyes, narrow and hot in his gaunt dark face, flashed a desperate look at the small flyer from which he had just been taken.

It bobbed on the heaving mud, mocking him. The eight-foot Europan guard standing between it and MacVickers made a slow weaving motion with his tentacles.

MacVickers studied the Europan with the hating eyes of a wolf in a trap. His smooth black body had a dull sheen of red under the Jupiter-light. There was no back nor front to him, no face. Only the four long rubbery legs, the roundish body, and the tentacles in a waving crown above.

MacVickers bared white, uneven teeth. His big bony fists clenched. He took one step toward the Europan.

A tentacle flicked out, daintily, and touched the silver collar at the Earthman's throat. Raw electric current, generated in the Europan's body, struck into him, a shuddering, blinding agony surging down his spine.

He stumbled backward, and his foot went off into emptiness. He twisted blindly, catching the opposite side of the shaft, and hung there, groping with his foot for the ladder rungs, cursing in a harsh, toneless voice.

The tentacle struck out again, with swift, exquisite skill. Three times like a red-hot lash across his face, and twice, harder, across his hands. Then it touched the collar again.

MacVickers retched and let go. He fell jarringly down the ladder, managed to break his fall onto the metal floor below, and crouched there, sick and furious and afraid.

The hatch cover clanged down over him like the falling hammer of doom.

*

MacVickers dropped into a circular room thirty feet across, floored and walled with metal and badly lighted. The roof was of thick glassite plates. Through them, very clearly, MacVickers could see four Europan guards, watching.

"They're always there," said the Venusian softly. "You'll come to love them, stranger."

There were men standing around the ladder foot, thirteen of them, with the Venusian. Earthmen, Martians, Venusians, pale, stark naked, smeared with a blue-green stain. Their muscles stood out sharp on their gaunt bodies, their silver collars a mocking note of richness.

Deep, deep, inside himself, MacVickers shivered. His nostrils wrinkled. There was fear in the room. The smell of it, the shudder of it in the air. Fear that was familiar and accustomed, lying in uneasy sleep, but ready to awake.

There were other men, four or five of them, back in the shadows by the wall bunks. They didn't speak, nor come out.

He took a deep breath and said steadily, "I'm Chris MacVickers. Deep-space trader out of Terra. They caught me trying to get through the Asteroid lines."

Their eyes glistened at him, looking from him to something behind them that he couldn't see. They were waiting, and there was something ghoulish in it.

The Venusian said sharply, "Tough luck, MacVickers. I'm Loris, late of the Venusian Guard. Introduce yourselves, boys."

They did, in jerky detached voices, their eyes sliding from him to the hidden something. Loris drew a little closer, and one of the Earthmen in the group came toward him.

"I'm Pendleton," he said. "The *Starfish*. Remember?"

MacVickers stared at him. The furrows deepened in his craggy face. He said, "My God!" very softly, and not as a curse. "Pendleton!"

The man grinned wryly. He was English, the ravaged ghost of the big, ruddy, jovial spaceman MacVickers remembered.

"Quite a change, eh? Well, perhaps we're lucky, MacVickers. We shan't have to see the smash."

MacVickers' head dropped forward. "Then you saw it coming, too?"

Loris made a little bitter laugh that was almost a sob. All the desperate boyish humor was gone from his face, leaving it old and grim.

"Who hasn't? I've been here—God knows. An eternity. But even before my ship was taken, we knew it. We can't build spaceships as fast as their Jovium destroys them. When they break through the Asteroid line...."

Pendleton's quiet voice was grave. "Mars is old and tired and torn with famine. Venus is young, but her courage is undisciplined. Her barbarians aren't suited to mechanized warfare. And Earth...." He sighed. "Perhaps if we hadn't fought so much among ourselves...."

MacVickers said harshly, "It wouldn't make much difference. When a man has a weapon that causes metal to explode its own atoms, it doesn't make any difference what you stack up against him."

He shook his craggy head impatiently. "What is this place? What are you doing here? The Jovies just brought me here and dumped me in without a word of explanation."

Pendleton shrugged. "We, too. There's a pit below, full of machinery. We work it, but we're not told why. Of course, we do a lot of guessing."

"Guessing!" The word rose sharp on the thick hot air. A man burst out of the group and stood swaying with the restless motion of the floor. He was a swart Low-Canal Martian. His yellow cat-eyes glittered in his hatch-face, and his thin ropy muscles twitched.

"I'll tell you what this place is, Earthman. It's a hell! And we're caught in it. Trapped, for the rest of our lives." He turned on Pendleton. "It's your fault. We were in a neutral port. We might have been safe. But you had to get back...."

"Janu!" Pendleton's voice cracked like a whip. The Martian went silent, watching him. There was more than hate in his yellow eyes. *Dando*, the beginning of the trap-madness. MacVickers had seen it in men who couldn't stand the confinement of a deep-space voyage.

The Englishman said quietly, "Janu was my glory-hole foreman. He rather holds this against me."

The Martian snarled, and then coughed. The cough became a paroxysm. He stumbled away, grey-faced and twitching, bent almost double.

"It's the heat," said Loris, "and the damp. Poor devil."

*

MacVickers thought of the air of Mars, cold and dry and pure. The floor rocked under him. Eyes, with the queer waiting shine to them, slid furtively to the hidden thing behind the standing men.

The hot wet air lay on his lungs. He sweated. There was a stir of nausea in him and the lights swirled. He shut his jaw hard.

He said, "What did Janu mean, the rest of our natural lives? They'll let us go when the war's over—if there's anything left to go to."

There was a tight little silence. And then, from the shadows against the wall, there came a brittle, whispering laugh.

"The war? They let us go before that!"

The group parted. MacVickers had a brief glimpse of a huge man crouched in a strange position on the floor. Then he couldn't see anything but the shape that came slowly out into the light.

It moved with a stiff, tottering gait, and its naked feet made a dry clicking sound on the metal floor. MacVickers' hand closed hard on the ladder behind him.

It had been a man, an Earthman. His body was still tall, his features still fine. But there was a film over him, a pale blue-green sheathe that glistened dully.

He thrust out an arm, with a hand on it like a hand carved in aquamarine. "Touch it," he whispered.

MacVickers touched it. It was quite hard, and warm only with the heat of the air. MacVickers' grey-green eyes met the sunken, sheathed eyes of the Earthman. His body hurt with the effort to control it.

"When we can no longer move," the whispering voice said, "they take us up the shaft and throw us over, into the mud. That's why you're here—because we were one man short."

MacVickers put his hand back on the ladder rung. "How long?"

OUTPOST ON IO

"About three Earth months."

He looked at the blue-green stain that smeared them all. The color of the mud. His hands sweated on the ladder rung. "What is it?"

"Something in the mud. A radioactivity, I think. It seems to turn the carbon in human flesh to a crystalline form. You become a living jewel. It's painless. But it's...." He didn't finish.

Beads of sweat stood on MacVickers' forehead. The men standing watching him smiled a little. There was motion behind them. Loris and Pendleton stiffened, and their eyes met.

MacVickers said steadily, "I don't understand. The mud's outside."

Loris said, with a queer, hurried urgency, "You will. It's almost time for the other shift...."

He broke off. Men scattered suddenly, crouching back in a rough circle, grinning with feral nervousness. The room was suddenly quiet.

The crouching man had risen. He stood with his huge corded legs wide apart, swaying with the swaying of the floor, his round head sunk between ridges of muscle, studying the Earthman out of pale, flat eyes.

Loris put his old, bitter boy's face close to MacVickers. His whisper was almost inaudible.

"Birek. He's boss here. He's mad. Don't fight him."

II

MacVickers' grey-green eyes narrowed. He didn't move. Birek breathed in slow, deep sighs. He was a Venusian, a coal-swamper from his size and pallor and the filthy-white hair clubbed in his neck.

He shimmered, very faintly in the dim light. The first jewel-crust was forming across his skin.

Knife-sharp and startling across the silence, a round hatch-cover in the floor clashed open. Sweat broke cold on MacVickers. Men began to come out of the hole, just at the edge of his vision. Naked, dirty men with silver collars.

They had been talking, cursing, jostling. The first ones saw Birek and stopped, and the silence trickled back down the shaft. It was utterly quiet again, except for the harsh straining of lungs against the hot, wet air and the soft sounds of naked men climbing the ladder.

The cords ridged on MacVickers' jaw. He shifted his balance slightly, away from the ladder. He could see the faces thrust forward in the dim light, eager, waiting.

Shining eyes, shining teeth, cheek-bones shining with sweat. Frightened, suffering men, watching another man fear and suffer, and being glad about it.

Birek moved forward, slowly. His eyes held a pale glitter, like distant ice, and his lips smiled.

"I prayed," he said softly. "I was answered. You, new man! Get down on your belly."

Loris grinned at Birek, but there was no humor in his eyes. He had drawn a little away from MacVickers. He said carelessly:

"There's no time for that now, Birek. It's our shift. They'll be burning us if we don't go."

Birek repeated, "Down on your belly," not looking at Loris.

A vein began to throb on MacVickers' forehead. He looked slight, almost small against the Venusian's huge bulk.

He said quietly, "I'm not looking for trouble.

"Then get down."

"Sorry," said MacVickers. "Not today."

Pendleton's voice cracked out sharply. "Let him alone, Birek! You men, down the ladder! They're going for the shockers."

MacVickers was aware of movement overhead, beyond the glass roof. Men began to drop slowly, reluctantly, down the ladder. There was sweat on Pendleton's forehead and Loris' face was as grey as his eyes.

Birek said hoarsely, "Down! Grovel! Then you can go."

"No." The ladder was beyond Birek. There was no way past him.

Loris said, in a swift harsh whisper, "Get down, MacVickers. For God's sake get down, and then come on!"

MacVickers shook his head stubbornly. The giant smiled. There was something horribly wrong about that smile. It was the smile of a man in agony when he feels the anaesthetic taking hold. Peaceful, and happy.

He struck out, startlingly fast for such a big man. MacVickers shrank aside. The fist grazed past his head, tearing his ear. He crouched and went in, trying for a fast body-blow and a sidestep.

He'd forgotten the glimmering sheathe. His fist struck Birek on the mark, and it was like striking glass that didn't shatter. The pain shot up his arm, numbing, slowing, sickening. Blood spattered out from his knuckles.

Birek's right swept in, across the side of his head.

MacVickers went down, on his right side. Birek put a foot in the small of his back. "Down," he said. "Grovel."

MacVickers twisted under the foot, snarling. He brought up his own feet, viciously, with all his strength. The pain of impact made him whimper, but Birek staggered back, thrown off balance.

There was no sign of hurt in his face. He stood there, looking down at MacVickers. Suddenly, shockingly, he was crying. He made no sound. He didn't move. But the tears ran out of his eyes.

A deep, slow shudder shook MacVickers. He said softly, "There's no pain, is there?"

Birek didn't speak. The tears glistened over the faint, hard film on his cheeks. MacVickers got up slowly. The furrows were deep and harsh in his face and his lips were white.

Loris pulled at him. Somewhere Pendleton's voice was yelling, "Hurry! Hurry, *please!*"

*

The guards were doing something overhead. There was a faint crackling sound, a flicker of sparks in a circle around the top of the wall. Shivering, tingling pain swept through MacVickers from the silver collar at his throat.

Men began to whisper and curse. Loris clawed at him, shoved him down the ladder, kicked his face to make him hurry. The pain abated.

MacVickers looked up. The great corded legs of Birek were coming down, the soles of the feet making a faint, hard sound on the rungs.

The hatch closed overhead. The voice of the dying Earthman came dry and soft over his shoulder.

"Here's where you'll work until you die. How do you like it?"

MacVickers turned, scowling. It was hot. The room above was cool by comparison. The air was thick and sluggish with the reek of heated oil and metal. It was a big space, running clear to the curving wall, but the effect was of stifling, cramped confinement.

Machinery crammed the place, roaring and hissing and clattering, running in a circuit from huge intake pumps through meaningless bulking shapes to a forced-air outlet, with oil-pumps between them.

The pumps brought mud into a broad sluice, and the blue-green stain of it was everywhere.

There were two glassite control boxes high on the walls, each with a black, tentacled Europan. About five feet overhead was a system of metal catwalks giving complete coverage of the floor area. There were Europans on the walks, too, eight of them, patrolling steadily.

Their sleek, featureless bodies were safe from contact with the mud. They carried heavy plastic tubes in their tentacles, and there were heavy-duty shockers mounted at every intersection.

MacVickers grinned dourly. "Trustful lot."

"Very." Pendleton nudged him over toward a drive motor attached to some kind of a centrifugal separator. Loris and the blue-sheathed Earthman followed, with Birek coming slowly behind him.

MacVickers said, "What's all this for?"

Pendleton shook his head. "We don't know. But we have an idea that Jovium comes from the mud."

"Jovium!" MacVickers' grey-green eyes began to grow hot. "The stuff that's winning this war for them. The metal destroyer!"

"We're not sure, of course." Pendleton's infinitely weary eyes turned across the stretch of greasy metal deck to the end of the circuit. "But look there. What does that suggest to you?"

The huge pipe of the forced-air ejector ran along the deck there behind a screen of heavy metal mesh. Just above it, enclosed behind three thicknesses of glassite, was a duct leading upward. The duct, from the inordinate size of its supports and its color, was pure lead.

Lead. Lead pipe, lead armor. Radiations that changed living men into half-living diamonds. Nobody knew what Jovium was or where it came from—only it did.

But scientists on the three besieged worlds thought it was probably an isotope of some powerful radioactive metal, perhaps uranium, capable of setting up a violent progressive breakdown in metallic atoms.

"If," said MacVickers softly, "the pipe were lined with plastic....Blue mud! I've traded through these moons, and the only other deposit of that mud is a saucepanful on J-XI! This must be their only source."

Loris shoved an oil can at him. "What difference does it make?" he said savagely.

MacVickers took the can without seeing it. "They store it up there, then, in the space between the inner wall and the outer. If somebody could get up there and set the stuff off...."

Pendleton's mouth twisted. "Can you see any way?"

He looked. Guards and shockers, charged ladders and metal screens. No weapons, no place to conceal them anyway. He said doggedly:

"But if someone could escape and get word back....This contraption is a potential bomb big enough to blow Io out of space! The experts think it only takes a fraction of a gram of the pure stuff to power a disintegrator shell."

There was a pulse beating hard under his jaw and his grey-green eyes were bright.

Loris said, "Escape." He said it as though it were the most infinitely beautiful word in existence, and as though it burned his mouth.

"Escape," whispered the man with the shimmering, deadly sheathe of aquamarine. "There is no escape but—this."

*

MacVickers said, into the silence that followed, "I'm going to try. One thing or the other, I'm going to try."

Pendleton's incredibly tired eyes looked at the livid burns on MacVickers' face. "It's been tried. And it's no use."

Birek moved suddenly out of his queer, dazed stillness. He looked up and made a hoarse sound in his throat. MacVickers caught a

15

flicker of motion overhead, but he didn't pay attention to it. He went on, speaking quietly in a flat, level voice.

"There's a war on. We're all in it. Soldiers, civilians, and kings, the big fellows and the little ones. When I got my master's ticket, they told me a man's duty wasn't done until his ship was cradled or he was dead.

"My ship's gone. But I haven't died, yet."

Pendleton's broad, gaunt shoulders drooped. He turned his head away. Loris' face was a death-mask carved from grey bone. He said, almost inaudibly:

"Shut up, damn you. Shut up."

The movement was closer overhead, ominously close. The men scattered across the pit had stopped working, watching MacVickers with glistening, burning eyes across hot oil-filmed metal.

MacVickers said harshly, "I know what's wrong with you. You were broken before you came, thinking the smash was coming and it was no use."

Pendleton whispered, "You don't know, the things they do to you."

Stiff and dry out of the Earthman's aquamarine mask, came the words, "You'll learn. There's no hope, MacVickers, and the men have all they can bear without pain.

"If you bring them more suffering, MacVickers, they'll kill you."

Heat. Oil and reeking metal, and white stiff faces filmed with sweat. Eyes shining, hot and glittering with fear. Rocking floor and sucking pumps and a clutching nausea in his belly. Birek, standing straight and still, watching him. Watching. Everybody, watching.

MacVickers put his hand flat on the engine-housing beside him. "There's more to it than duty," he said softly, and smiled, without humor, the vertical lines deep in his cheeks. His gaunt Celtic head had a grim beauty.

His voice rang clear across the roar of the machines. "I'm Christopher Rory MacVickers. I'm the most important thing in the universe. And if I have to give my life, it'll not be without return on the value of it!"

Janu the Martian, away on the other side of the pit, made a shrill wailing cry. Loris and Pendleton flinched away like dogs afraid of the whip, looking upward.

MacVickers glimpsed a dark tentacled shape on the catwalk above, just before the shattering electricity coursed through him. He screamed, once. And then Birek moved.

He struck Loris and Pendleton and the blue-sheathed Earthman out of the way like children. His left leg took MacVickers behind the knees in the same instant that his right hand pushed MacVickers' face.

MacVickers fell heavily on his back, screaming at the contact of the metal floor. Then Birek sprawled over him, shielding his body with the bulk of his own.

The awful shocking pain was lessened. Lying there, looking up into Birek's pale eyes, MacVickers made his twitching lips say, "Why?"

Birek smiled. "The current doesn't hurt much any more. And I want you for myself—to break."

MacVickers drew a deep, shuddering breath and smiled back, the lines deep in his lean cheeks.

*

He had no clear memories of that shift. Heat and motion and strangling air, and Janu coughing with a terrible, steady rhythm, his own hands trying to guide the oil can. Toward the end of the time he fainted, and it was Birek who carried him up the ladder.

He had no way of knowing how long after that he came to. There was no time in that little hell. The first thing he noticed, with the hair-trigger senses of a man trained to ships, that the motion of the room was different.

He sat up straight on the bunk where Birek had laid him. "The tidal wave," he said, over a quick stab of fear. "What...."

"We ride it out," said Loris bitterly. "We always have."

MacVickers knew the Jovian Moons pretty well. Remembering the tremendous tides and winds caused by the gravitational pull of Jupiter, he shuddered. There was no solid earth on Io, nothing but mud. And the extraction plant, from the feel of it, was a hollow bell sunk under it, perfectly free.

It had to be free. No mooring cable made could stand the pull of a Jupiter-tide.

"One thing about it," said Pendleton with quiet viciousness. "It makes the bloody Jovies seasick."

Janu the Martian made a cracked, harsh laugh. "So they keep a weak current on us all the time." His hatchet-face was drawn, his yellow cat-eyes lambent in the dim light.

The men sprawled on their bunks, not talking much. Birek sat on the end of his, watching MacVickers with his pale still eyes. There was a tightness in the room.

It was coming. They were going to break him now, before he hurt them. Break him, or kill him.

MacVickers wiped the sweat from his face and said, "I'm thirsty."

Pendleton pointed to a thing like a horse-trough against the bulkhead. His eyes were tired and very sad. Loris was scowling at his stained and faintly filmed feet.

There wasn't much water in the trough. What there was was brackish and greasy. MacVickers drank and splashed some on his face and body. He saw that he was already stained with the mud. It wouldn't wash off.

The dying Earthman whispered, "There is food also."

MacVickers looked at the basket of spongy synthetic food, and shook his head.

The floor dipped and swung. There was a frightening, playful violence about it, like the first soft taps of a tiger's paw. Loris looked up at the glass roof with the black shapes beyond.

"They get the pure air," he said. "Our ventilator pipes are only a few inches wide, lest we crawl up through them."

Pendleton said, rather loudly, "The swine breathe through the skin, you know. All their sense organs, sight and hearing...."

"Shut up," snarled Janu. "Stop talking for time."

The sprawled men on the bunks drew themselves slowly tight, breathing hard and deep in anticipation. And Birek rose.

MacVickers faced them, Birek and the rest. There was no lift in his heart. He was cold and sodden, like a chuted ox watching the poleaxe fall. He said, with a bitter, savage quiet,

"You're a lot of bloody cowards. You, Birek. You're scared of the death creeping over you, and the only way you can forget the fear is to make someone else suffer.

"It's the same with all of you. You have to trample me down to your own level, break me for the sake of your souls as much as your bodies."

He looked at the numbers of them, at Birek's huge impervious bulk and his great fists. He touched his silver collar, remembering the agony of the shock through it.

"And I will break. You know that, damn you."

He gave back three paces and set his feet. "All right. Come on, Birek. Let's get it over with."

*

OUTPOST ON IO

The Venusian came toward him across the heaving floor. Loris still looked at his feet and Pendleton's eyes were agonized. MacVickers wiped his hands across his buttocks. The palms were filmed and slick with oil from the can he had handled.

There was no use to fight. Birek was twice his size, and he couldn't be hurt anyway. The diamond-sheathe even screened off the worst of the electric current, being a non-conductor.

That gave the dying men an advantage. But even if they had spirit enough left by that time to try anything, the hatches were still locked tight by air-pressure and the sheer numbers of their suffering mates would pull them down. Also, the Jovies were as strong as four men.

Non-conductor. Sheathed skin. Birek's shoulders tensing for the first blow. Sweat trying to break through the film of oil on his palms, the slippery feel of his hands as he clenched them.

Birek's fist lashed out. MacVickers dodged under it, looking for an opening, dreading the useless agony of impact. The bell lurched wildly.

A guard moved abruptly overhead. The motion caught MacVickers' eye. Something screamed sharply in his head: Pendleton's voice saying, "They breathe through the skin. All their sense organs...."

He sensed rather than saw Birek's fist coming. He twisted, enough to take the worst of it on his shoulder. It knocked him halfway across the deck. And then the current came on.

It was weak, but it made him jerk and twitch. He scrambled up on the pitching deck and started to speak. Birek was coming again, leisurely, smiling. Then, quite suddenly, the hatch cover clanged open, signalling the change of the shifts. MacVickers stood still for a second. Then he laughed, a queer little chuckle, and made a rush for the hatch.

III

He went down it with Birek's hand brushing past his head. Men yelled and cursed. He trampled on them ruthlessly. The ones lower down fell off the ladder to avoid his feet.

There was a clamor up above. Hands grabbed at him. He lashed out, kicking and butting. His rush carried him through and out across the pit, toward the space between the end points of the horseshoe circuit.

He slowed down, then. The guards had noticed the scuffle. But it seemed to be only the shift changing, and MacVickers looked like a man going peacefully for oil.

Peacefully. The blood thundered in his head, he was cold, and the skin of his back crawled. Men shoved and swore back by the ladder. He went on, not too fast, fighting the electric shiver in his brain.

Fuel and lubricating oils were brought up, presumably from tanks in a still lower level, by big pressure pumps. All three sets of pumps, intake, outlet, and oil, worked off the same compressed-air unit.

He set the lubricating-oil pump going and rattled cans into place. The men of his shift were straggling out from the ladder, twitching from the light current, scared, angry, but uncertain.

There was a subtle change in the attitude of the Europan guards. Their movements were sluggish, faintly uncertain. MacVickers grinned viciously. Seasick. They'd be sicker—if they didn't get him too soon.

The surging pitch of the bell was getting worse. The tide was rising, and the mud was playing with the bell like a child throwing a ball. Nausea began to clutch at MacVickers' stomach.

The pressure-gage on the pump was rising. He let it rise, praying, his grey-green eyes hot and bright. Going with the motion of the deck, he sprawled over against the intake pumps.

21

He spun the wheel on the pressure-control as far as it would go. A light wrench, chained so that it could not be thrown, lay at his feet. He picked it up, his hand jerking and tingling, and began to work at the air-pipe coupling.

Hands gripped his shoulder suddenly, slewing him around. The yellow eyes of Janu the Martian glared into his.

"What are you doing here, Earthman? This is my station."

Then he saw the pressure gauge. He let out a keening wail, cut short by the crunch of MacVickers' fist on his mouth. MacVickers whirled and swung the wrench.

The loose coupling gave. Air burst whistling from the pipe, and the rhythm of the pumps began to break.

But Janu's cry had done it. Men were pelting toward him, and the guards were closing in overhead.

MacVickers flung himself bodily on the short hose of the oil-pump.

Birek, Loris, Pendleton, the dying Earthman, the hard faces behind them. The guards were manning the shockers. Up in the control boxes black tentacles were flashing across banks of switches. He had to work fast, before they cut the pressure.

Birek was ahead of the others, very close. MacVickers gave him the oil-stream full in the face. It blinded him. Then the nearest shocker came on, focussed expertly on MacVickers.

He shut his teeth hard, whimpering through them, and turned the hard forced stream of oil into the hoarsely shrieking blast from the open pipe.

Oil sprayed up in a heavy, blinding fog. Burning, shuddering agony shook MacVickers, but he held his hose, his feet braced wide, praying to stand up long enough.

The catwalks were hidden in the oily mist. The ventilating blowers caught it, thrusting it across the whole space. MacVickers yelled through it, his voice hardly recognizable as human.

"You, out there! All of you. This is your chance. Are you going to take it?"

Something fell, close by, with a heavy thrashing thud. Something black and tentacled and writhing, covered with a dull film.

MacVickers laughed, and the laughter was less human than the voice.

"Cowards!" he cried. "All right. I'll do it all myself."

Somebody yelled, "They're dying. Look!" There was another heavy thud. The hot strangling fog roiled with hidden motion. MacVickers gasped and retched and shuddered helplessly. He was going to drop the hose in a minute. He was going to fall down and scream.

If they stepped the power up one more notch, he was going to fall down and die. Only they were dying too, and forgetting about power.

It seemed a static eternity to MacVickers, but it had all happened in the space of a dozen heartbeats. There were yells and shouts and a sort of animal tumult in the thick haze. Suddenly Pendleton's voice rang out of it.

"MacVickers! I'm with you, man! You others, listen. He's giving us the break we needed. Don't let him down!"

And Janu screamed, "No! He's killed the guards, but there are more. They'll fry us from the control boxes if we help him."

The pressure was dropping in the pipe as the power cut out. There was a last hiss, a spurt of oily spray, then silence. MacVickers dropped the hose.

Janu's voice went on, sharp and harsh with fear. "They'll fry us, I tell you. We'll lie here and jerk and scream until we're crazy. I'm going to die. I know it. But I won't go through that, for nothing! I'm going back by the ladder and pray they won't notice me."

More sounds, more tumult. Men suddenly torn between hope and abject terror. MacVickers said wearily into the fog,

"If you help me, we can win the war for our worlds. Destroy this bell, start the Jovium working, destroy Io—victory for us. And if you don't, I hope you fry here and in Hell afterward."

They wavered. MacVickers could hear their painful breathing, ragged with the emotion in them. Some of them started toward the sound of Pendleton's voice.

Janu made an eerie wauling sound, like a hurt cat, and went for him.

*

MacVickers started to help, but the current froze him to the metal floor. He strained, feeling his nerves, his brain dissolving in a shuddering fire. He knew why the others had broken so soon. The current did things to you, inside.

He couldn't see what was happening. The heavy mist choked his eyes, his throat, his nostrils. The pitching of the bell was a nightmare thing. Men thrashed and struggled and cursed.

So he had killed the guards. So what. There were still the control boxes. If they didn't rush them before the oil settled, they wouldn't have a chance.

Why not give up? Let himself dissolve into the blackness he was fighting off?

A great pale shape came striding through the mist toward him. Birek. This was it, then. Well, he'd had his moment of fun. His fists came up in a bland, instinctive gesture.

Birek laughed. The current made him jerk only a little, in his thin diamond sheathe. He bunched his shoulders and reached out.

MacVickers felt himself ripped clear of the floor. In a second he was out of focus of the shocker and the pain was gone. He came nearest to fainting then, but Birek's huge hand shook him by the hair and Birek's voice shouted,

"Tell 'em, little man! Tell 'em it's better to die quick, now, than go mad with fear."

"Come on!" yelled Pendleton. "Here's our chance to show we're still men. Hurry up, you sons!"

MacVickers looked at the Venusian's face. The terrible frozen fear was gone from his eyes. He wanted to die, now, quickly, fighting for vengeance.

The gray, pinched face of Loris loomed abruptly out of the fog. It was suddenly young again, and the smile was genuine. He said,

"Let's teach 'em to mind, Birek. MacVickers, I...." He shook his head, looking away. "You know."

"I know. Hurry up with it."

Pendleton's voice burst out of the fog, triumphantly. Janu crouched on the heaving deck, bleeding and whimpering. MacVickers yelled,

"Who's with me? We're going to take the control boxes. Who wants to be a hero?"

Birek laughed and threw him bodily up onto the catwalk overhead. Most of the men came forward then. The three or four that were left looked at the Martian and followed.

Birek helped them up onto the catwalk. They were moving, now. It took only a few seconds. MacVickers divided them into two groups.

"You men that are sheathed go first, to help block the charge. It'll be your job to take the Jovies out of the way. Quick, before this fog settles enough so they can see to focus on us."

They split up, running along the walk that connected with the control boxes, hurdling the bodies of Jovians suffocated in oil. Presently the glassite door loomed before them.

Birek and the dying Earthman led MacVickers' party. The Venusian wrenched open the door. And MacVickers felt his heart stop.

There were three Europans instead of one. The guards had come down from above.

"Get them out here," he said. "Out into the oil."

A wave of shuddering agony tossed through him. The Jovies were using their powerful hand-tubes. Only the glassite walls partially protected them.

The fog began to whip past him. He groaned, thinking that it was going. And then he put his head in his hands and wept with incredulous, thankful joy.

The oily mist was being sucked into the box by powerful ventilators. MacVickers remembered Loris saying, "They get the pure air. Our ventilator tubes are only a few inches wide."

He laughed. The bell swooped sickeningly. Somewhere off in the fog he heard screams and shouts and Pendleton's voice roaring triumph.

He thought, "We never could have done it if the tide hadn't come and made the Jovies seasick."

He laughed again. It tickled him that seasickness should lose a war.

IV

They went in and up the ladders into the sealed storage space next the convict quarters. There was a huge cylinder of lead suspended over the mouth of the duct from the extractor.

"They must collect the stuff when they bring oil and supplies," said Loris. "Well, MacVickers, what happens to us now?"

MacVickers looked at them, the lines deep in his face. "We all agree, don't we, that there's no hope of escape? If we wait until the next supply ship comes and try to take it, we lose the chance of doing—well, call it our duty if you want to. That is, to wreck their only source of the explosive that's winning the war for them.

"I think you know," he added, "what our chances of taking that ship would be, without offensive weapons or any protection against theirs. It would only mean a return to this slavery, if they didn't kill us all outright."

His grey-green eyes were somber, deeply bright.

"It comes down to this. Shall we turn this bell into a disintegrator bomb, setting the Jovium free to destroy its own and every other metallic atom in the mud, or shall we gamble our worlds on the slim chance of saving our necks?"

Loris looked down at the deck and said softly, "Why should we worry about our necks, MacVickers? You've saved our souls."

"Agreed, then, all you men?"

Birek looked them over. "The man who refuses will have no neck to save," he said.

There was no disagreement.

MacVickers turned to the leaden cylinder. It was fixed to the duct by a plastic-lined, lead-sheathed collar. There was an arrangement whereby a plug could be driven into the open mouth of the filled cylinder without spilling a grain of the stuff.

MacVickers reached up and loosed the apparatus that held the cylinder upright. It fell over with a shattering crash. A palely glowing powder puffed out, settling over the adjacent metal.

OUTPOST ON IO

MacVickers had one second of terror. An eerie bluish light grew, throwing faces into strong relief. Pendleton, praying silently. Loris, smiling. The blue-sheathed Earthman with closed eyes, his face a mask of peace. The others, facing a death they understood and welcomed. All of them, thinking of three little worlds that could go on living their own lives.

Birek grinned at him. "I'm glad you ran away," he whispered.

MacVickers grinned back.